THIS BAD MOOD
BELONGS TO:

Little, Brown and Company
Hachette Book Group
1290 Avenue of the Americas, New York, NY 10104
Visit us at lb-kids.com
Little, Brown and Company is a division of Hachette Book Group, Inc.
The Little, Brown name and logo are trademarks of Hachette Book Group, Inc.
The publisher is not responsible for websites (or their content) that are not owned by the publisher.

First Edition: October 2017
ISBNs: 978-0-316-39278-5 (hardcover), 978-0-316-39276-1 (ebook)
10 9 8 7 6 5 4 3 2 1
1010
PRINTED IN CHINA

ABOUT THIS BOOK

The illustrations for this book were done in gouache, colored ink, and pencil. This book was edited by Susan Rich and designed by David Caplan and Nicole Brown. The production was supervised by Ruiko Tokunaga, and the production editor was Jen Graham. The text was set in Futura, and the display type is hand lettered.

The Bad Mood and the Stick

Lemony Snicket

Art by Matthew Forsythe

 Little, Brown and Company
New York   Boston

Once there was a stick and a bad mood.

The stick was on the ground,

and the bad mood was with a girl named Curly.

Curly had been with the bad mood for two hours, since she had seen an ice cream store but hadn't gotten any ice cream.

The stick had been on the ground since
last night, when the tree dropped it.

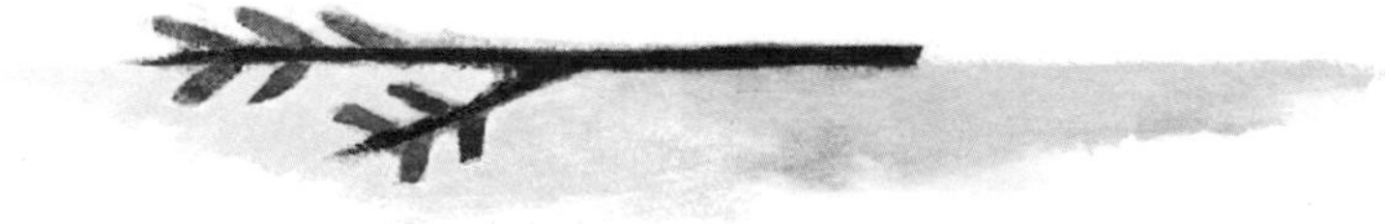

Curly picked up the stick and used it to poke her brother.

"That's not nice," said her mother. "Apologize to Napoleon, and throw the stick in the bushes."

Curly had really enjoyed poking her brother Napoleon—
so much that her bad mood was gone.

Her mother was carrying it now. "Harrumph," she said, which is a bad mood noise.

The stick didn't say anything,

even when a raccoon picked it up.

Who knows what the raccoon wanted to do with the stick,

but he ran out of the bushes
and frightened an old man
named Lou.

"Holy moly!" said Lou, which is what he
always said when something exciting
happened, and his feet did a little dance,

and he fell into a puddle.

Curly's mother couldn't help herself and started to laugh.

Her bad mood was gone.

Lou had it.

The sound of all that laughter startled the raccoon, and he dropped the stick in the mud.

"Look at my pants," Lou said, which was *his* bad mood noise. "They're a muddy awful mess."

The stick didn't answer.

Lou went right to the dry cleaner's. A lady named Mrs. Durham was head of the establishment, with a pencil behind her ear.

"Take that pencil outta your ear," said Lou. "You gotta wash these pants and wash them quick. I'll stand around here in my underwear until you're done."

"You will do no such thing," said Mrs. Durham. "This is a family place."

But Lou already had his pants off. "Here you go," he said. "They're a muddy awful mess."

"Ugh," said Mrs. Durham, looking at the pants and looking at Lou, and you would think that the bad mood would have moved on to her.

But it didn't.

She took one look at Lou in his underwear,
and the bad mood flew right out the window.

You never know what is going to happen.

Same thing with the stick. You would never guess, but some kind of bug made a brightly colored cocoon on it.

"Well, look at that," said Bert, and picked it up to look at it better.

He took it back to his ice cream store and put it on display.

"That's sure unusual," said Curly's mother, when they walked by. "Whattaya say, kids? Let's all have some ice cream."

Curly had fudge ripple, and Napoleon had mint chip. Curly's mother ordered vanilla yogurt, but then she changed her mind and had fudge ripple, too.

This didn't bother Bert. The bad mood was nowhere around.

By the time Lou arrived, with his pants all clean and pressed, he wanted a double scoop, and so did Mrs. Durham.

"Holy moly," Lou said, "do I love ice cream."

Mrs. Durham smiled. "Same here," she said,

and three years later they were married. The wedding was
right there in the park, and everyone in this book was invited.

Even the raccoon. Curly and Napoleon carried the flowers,
and they did great. You never know what is going to happen.

By then the bad mood had been all around the world.

You yourself had it several times.

The stick, however, stayed in the ice cream store.
The cocoon had opened a long time ago,
and Bert had helped the bug fly out into the world,

but the stick he kept right there. It put him in a good mood.